PETER SAM

Based on *The Railway Series* by the Rev. W. Awdry

Illustrations by
Robin Davies and Jerry Smith

EGMONT

EGMONT

We bring stories to life

First published in Great Britain in 2005
by Egmont UK Limited
239 Kensington High Street, London W8 6SA
This edition published in 2008
All Rights Reserved

HiT entertainment

ISBN 978 1 4052 3470 2
3 5 7 9 10 8 6 4
Printed in Italy

FSC
Mixed Sources
Product group from well-managed
forests and other controlled sources

Cert no. TT-COC-002332
www.fsc.org
© 1996 Forest Stewardship Council

Egmont is passionate about helping to preserve the world's remaining ancient forests.
We only use paper from legal and sustainable forest sources.

This book is made from paper certified by the Forestry Stewardship Council (FSC),
an organisation dedicated to promoting responsible management of forest resources.
For more information on the FSC, please visit www.fsc.org. To learn more about
Egmont's sustainable paper policy, please visit www.egmont.co.uk/ethical

TO THE TRAINS ➡

This is a story about Peter Sam, a Narrow-Gauge Engine. He first worked at the Old Railway for The Thin Controller many years ago. Everyone made fun of his new funnel, but he soon had the last laugh …

It was winter on the Island of Sodor. Peter Sam was puffing slowly along the track.

He was worried about his funnel. It had not felt right since he had had an accident with some trucks, and now it felt like the wind was trying to blow it off.

"My funnel feels all wobbly," he said to his Driver. "I wish my new one would hurry up and arrive. The Thin Controller said it will be something special!"

"You and your special funnel," laughed Rusty, Sir Handel and Duncan. They all liked Peter Sam but his special funnel had become a bit of a joke.

The winter wind grew stronger and rain lashed down on the engines. The heavy rain turned the hillside streams into raging rivers which threatened to wash away the tracks.

Rusty worked hard carrying workmen up and down the line to clear the branches and leaves so the water could flow away from the tracks.

The next day, Rusty's Driver brought bad news. "There's been a washout near the tunnel," he said. "The track bed has been swept away. We need to repair it immediately!"

The repair work took much longer than expected. As the days went by, the weather became much colder and frosty. Finally, the repairs were finished so the tunnel could be used again.

The next morning, Peter Sam carefully went over the mended track and slowly rolled into the dark tunnel.

His Driver shouted, "There's something hanging from the roof!"

There was a loud clanging noise and Peter Sam suddenly felt rather strange. As he came out of the tunnel, his Driver saw that he had lost his funnel!

Peter Sam's Guard went back into the tunnel to find his funnel. He came out holding the funnel and a large icicle.

"This is what hit you!" he said. "We can't mend your funnel here, we'll have to finish the journey without it and get it repaired at the station."

Peter Sam set off again but, without his funnel, smoke billowed over the carriages and the passengers complained.

At the side of the track, his Driver noticed an old drainpipe. He wired it to Peter Sam to work as a funnel for the rest of the journey. Peter Sam was embarrassed.

"I hope none of the other engines see me looking like this," he said sadly.

But as Peter approached the station, Rusty and Sir Handel saw his drainpipe funnel. They burst into laughter and sang a song:

Peter Sam's said again and again,
His new funnel will put ours to shame.
But he went into a tunnel,
And lost his old funnel,
Now his famous special funnel's a drain!

Luckily for Peter Sam, his new funnel had arrived that day. He couldn't wait to see it, but when his Driver opened the parcel he thought there had been a mistake.

"Oh, no! Has somebody squashed my new funnel?" asked Peter Sam.

The Thin Controller laughed. "Don't worry," he said. "It's a special funnel, called a Giesl. It is the most up-to-date funnel there is!"

"How does it work?" asked Peter Sam.

"When you puff, you draw air through your fire to make it burn brightly. Your old funnel made puffin hard work, but your new Giesl funnel has special pipes to help the air come easily. You'll now have more strength to do your work."

Peter Sam wasn't sure that he was going to like having the strange new funnel.

At first, the other engines thought Peter Sam's new funnel was a great joke.

"Did you sit on it?" asked Duncan and hooted with laughter.

"It's certainly *special*!" giggled Sir Handel.

Peter Sam had wished he had his old funnel back but he soon realized that The Thin Controller had been right. His new funnel did make work much easier. Now the other engines would have nothing to laugh about.

Peter Sam became very proud of his new funnel. It helped him glide along the tracks, easily pulling long lines of trucks behind him.

Sir Handel, Duncan and Rusty soon stopped laughing at his new funnel. They watched in amazement as he sped past them, pulling more trucks than he had ever been able to before. The other engines wished they also had a special funnel just like Peter Sam!

TWO Great Offers for Thomas Fans!

In every Thomas Story Library book like this one, you will find a special token. Collect the tokens and claim exclusive Thomas goodies:

Offer 1

Collect 6 tokens and we'll send you a **poster** and a **bookmark** for only **£1**.
(to cover P&P)

For offer 1 please attach £1

Stick £1 coin here!

For offer 2 please attach £2

Stick £2 coin here!

1 THOMAS TOKEN · 1 THOMAS TOKEN ·

offer 2

Collect 12 tokens and we'll send you a choo-choo-tastic book bag for only £2.
(to cover P&P)

Visit **www.egmont.co.uk/thomaslibrary** for more special offers, games and competitions!

Simply tape a £1 or £2 coin in the space above, and fill in the form overleaf.

The Thomas bag contains 7 specially designed pockets to hold Thomas Story Library books. Please note that the books featured in the picture above are not included in the offer.

Reply Card for Thomas Goodies!

1 Yes, please send me a **Thomas poster and bookmark.**
I have enclosed **6 tokens plus a £1 coin** to cover P&P. ☐

2 Yes, please send me a **Thomas book bag.**
I have enclosed **12 tokens plus £2** to cover P&P. ☐

Simply fill in your details below and send them to:
Thomas Offers, PO BOX 715, Horsham, RH12 5WG

Fan's Name: ....

Address: ....

....

.... Date of Birth: ....

Email: ....

Name of parent/guardian: ....

Signature of parent/guardian: ....

Please allow 28 days for delivery. Offer is only available while stocks last. We reserve the right
to change the terms of this offer at any time and we offer a 14 day money back guarantee.
This does not affect your statutory rights. Offer applies to UK only. The cost applies to Postage
and Packaging (P&P).

We may occasionally wish to send you information about other Egmont children's books but if
you would rather we didn't please tick here ☐